When Jane-Marie Told My Secret

When Jane-Marie Told My Secret

by Gina Willner-Pardo
Illustrated by Nancy Poydar

Clarion Books/*New York*

Clarion Books
a Houghton Mifflin Company imprint
215 Park Avenue South, New York, NY 10003
Text copyright © 1995 by Gina Willner-Pardo
Illustrations copyright © 1995 by Nancy Poydar

The illustrations for this book were executed in watercolor
and colored pencil on paper.
The text was set in 14.5/19-point Goudy.

For information about permission to reproduce selections from this book,
write to Permissions, Houghton Mifflin Company,
215 Park Avenue South, New York, NY 10003.

Printed in the USA

Library of Congress Cataloging-in-Publication Data
Willner-Pardo, Gina.
When Jane-Marie told my secret / by Gina Willner-Pardo ;
illustrated by Nancy Poydar.
p. cm.
Summary: When Carolyn's best friend Jane-Marie tells her secret to someone else,
it makes a big difference in their friendship.
ISBN 0-395-66382-2
[1. Secrets—Fiction. 2. Friendship—Fiction.] I. Poydar, Nancy, ill. II. Title.
PZ7.W68368Wj 1995
[E]—dc20 94-12820
CIP
AC

WOZ 10 9 8 7 6 5 4 3 2 1

For Jim Killian, who has been helping me get the hang of it for years; and for Barb Hoversten, whose friendship is proof of the amazing and wonderful turns life can take.

G. W.-P.

For Susan, who practiced cartwheels with me.

N. P.

CONTENTS

1.
The Wrong Best Friend All Along

It started out just like any other day. I had oatmeal for breakfast. I left my lunch in Mrs. Newhart's car and had to run back to get it. I spelled everything right except *button*. At recess, I came in second in hopscotch.

But it wasn't like any other day. It was the day Jane-Marie told my secret.

We were walking home from school, the way we always did. We were going to Jane-Marie's house to practice gymnastics, which was our favorite thing to do.

"Did your mom buy celery?" I asked. We always had a snack of celery stuffed with peanut butter before practicing gymnastics. "Last time there wasn't any celery."

"I think so," Jane-Marie said. She sounded as if she wasn't sure.

Jane-Marie had been my best friend since pre-school. I could tell when she wasn't sure about things.

"Maybe we'd better practice at my house," I said. I knew we had celery.

"No," Jane-Marie said, "because Jason and Sam will hang around and shoot rubber bands at us."

"I guess," I said. My brothers can be very irritating. It was easier practicing gymnastics at Jane-Marie's. All she had was an older sister named Eloise, who knew how to drive and wouldn't let us in her room.

"Besides," Jane-Marie said, "we need a yard for cartwheels."

"That's true," I said. I live in an apartment. We don't have a yard.

Jane-Marie took off her backpack and set it on the curb. She did a cartwheel right there on the sidewalk. "How was that, CB?" she asked, standing up.

CB was my nickname, short for Carolyn Bennett, which is my real name. Only Jane-Marie called me CB.

"OK," I said, "except for your knees bending a little."

Jane-Marie sighed and pretended to look sad.

"I just can't get the hang of it," she said. Then she snuck a look at me and laughed.

I laughed, too. It was our favorite joke.

"What did one boy on the monkey bars say to the other boy on the monkey bars?" Jane-Marie would ask.

"What?"

"I can't get the hang of it!" We would laugh until our stomachs ached.

Jane-Marie picked up her backpack. We started walking again.

"Allison McNair does the best cartwheels in our class," Jane-Marie said.

"I think Katie Kempo's are the best," I said. I thought about my secret. I had only told it to Jane-Marie. I'd told her not to tell anyone because I would feel so stupid if anybody knew.

This was the secret: I wanted Katie Kempo to like me. I wasn't even sure why, except that she had pierced ears and went to soccer camp and everybody said she was the most popular girl in third grade.

Jane-Marie looked into the sun. Her eyes got squinty and she looked away.

"I heard that Katie Kempo never likes anyone who wants to be friends with her," Jane-Marie said. "Everyone says Katie doesn't like it when people try too hard to be her friend."

I looked at her. I couldn't believe it.

"You told my secret, didn't you?" I said.

"I don't think so," Jane-Marie said.

She sounded as if she wasn't sure at all.

"Who did you tell?" I asked.

Jane-Marie looked nervous. "I can't remember," she said.

I knew she was lying.

"You never said not to tell," she said.

Don't tell anyone, I'd said. Because I'd feel so stupid if anybody knew.

I started getting mad.

"It was a secret," I said. "Best friends are supposed to know about keeping secrets."

"Maybe we're not best friends anymore," Jane-Marie said.

Jane-Marie said stuff like that sometimes. Usually I didn't pay any attention. Jane-Marie always got over being mad.

But this was different. This time, *I* was mad.

I stopped walking. I thought about all that time since preschool when Jane-Marie had been my best friend.

Maybe, I thought, I've had the wrong best friend all along.

"I don't want to walk with you," I said. That wasn't what I wanted to say. But it was what came out.

Jane-Marie looked angry and embarrassed at the same time. I think she was hoping I would change my mind and walk with her.

But I didn't change my mind.

Pretty soon Jane-Marie got tired of waiting. She shrugged her shoulders and walked away. I could tell she was trying to look dignified.

I was pretty sure I would never get over being mad.

2.
No Going Back

"Carolyn?" Mom called as I slammed the front door. She was putting Sam in bed for a nap.

Mom works at home. She is a consultant, which means she talks on the phone a lot in between being a mom.

She tiptoed down the hall and followed me into the kitchen. "Weren't you going to Jane-Marie's?"

"Yes," I said.

Mom started to wash me an apple. "Change of plans?" she asked.

"Mm hm." I didn't want to talk about Jane-Marie. I wished Mom would go back to work.

But Mom is very smart. Also, very nosy. Consultants are supposed to ask a lot of questions, she always says.

"Carolyn? What's the matter?"

"Nothing," I said, looking at the floor.

Mom put the apple on a plate. She opened the refrigerator and pulled out milk.

"Are you sure?" she asked.

"Yes." I wondered if moms who weren't consultants asked this many questions.

Mom stuck her head back into the refrigerator. I could tell she was rummaging around.

"Do you want peanut butter and celery?" she asked.

I was still looking at the floor, but I couldn't see it, because the tears made everything seem blurry and far away. A few ran down my nose.

I heard the refrigerator door shut, and Mom's shoes clicking on the floor, and then I felt her arms around my head, and smelled her sweater.

I stayed that way a long time.

After a while, Mom stopped patting my hair and asked, "Do you want to tell me what happened?"

I took a deep breath. "I hate Jane-Marie," I said. "I hate her forever."

"Forever is a long time," Mom said.

"I don't care," I said. I didn't feel like agreeing. "Best friends are not supposed to tell your secret, or lie about who they told it to."

"No," said Mom. "They're not supposed to do those things."

"But they do," I said. "Being best friends is dumb."

"It's hard being best friends," Mom said. "It's complicated. Sometimes even best friends need time apart."

Hearing that made me think about tomorrow. Suddenly, I felt afraid. Tomorrow would be my first whole day of having no best friend.

It wasn't that I didn't have other friends. Gordon Breslow was my best friend when I stayed at my dad's. Once we built a fort in his mom's potting shed. But he didn't go to my school, so I only saw him in the summer.

Andrea White was my friend from Miss Ludlow's ballet class. She had a pink tutu with sparkles and was always doing handstands when Miss Ludlow wasn't looking. I really liked Andrea, but she was in the fourth grade. She was nice to me at school, but she had all the fourth graders to play with.

Eleanor Petersen was my second-best friend in third grade. We were always next to each other in class pictures because we were the same height. For her last birthday, Eleanor had a slumber party. We ate pizza and watched movies until Mr. Petersen said we were a disgrace to the neighborhood and made us turn out the lights.

The day after Jane-Marie told my secret, Eleanor and I met before school to work on math. Eleanor was terrible at math.

"I hate subtraction," she said. "It took me all of second grade just to figure out adding. Now this."

"It's not so hard," I said. "See? It's like adding. Only backwards."

I loved math. I loved that there were rules to follow. And that if you followed the rules, everything worked out.

Eleanor sighed. "I don't get number six," she said. "I did it over and over. It just wouldn't come out right."

I showed her how. While I was showing her, I wondered what kind of best friend Eleanor would be. Probably pretty good, I decided. She looked like the kind of person who would remember when something was supposed to be a secret.

The bell rang. We stood up. "I hate math," Eleanor said. "I just can't get the hang of it."

I felt as if somebody had kicked me in the stomach. I was somebody with no best friend. I had no one to call me a nickname. I had to remember old jokes alone.

The morning seemed as long as a week. I tried to concentrate. I was reading about Pilgrims when I felt a tap on my shoulder. I slid my hand behind my

seat and snatched the note Jane-Marie had stuck in the crack in my chair.

Almost not wanting to, I read Jane-Marie's note:

Are you still mad?

I wrote back:

Yes.

After a minute, I felt another tap. This time it felt more like a poke.

It was a dumb secret anyway.

Right then, I knew. There was no going back.

I wrote back:

Don't write me any more notes.

I half-turned in my seat. Enough to see Jane-Marie making a terrible face. A we're-not-friends-anymore face.

I ate lunch with Eleanor. We both had chocolate pudding in a cup and a banana and laughed at what a coincidence that was. I wondered if someday this would be one of our memories.

"What's your favorite food?" I asked her. It seemed funny to think about being best friends with someone and not know what her favorite food was. Jane-Marie's was lasagna with no mushrooms.

"French fries," Eleanor said.

It was a start.

I traded my corn chips for her coconut macaroons. And tried not to wonder what Jane-Marie was having for lunch.

3.
On the Way to Miss Ludlow's

"She was weird," Jason said. "You're better off without her."

He was walking me to Miss Ludlow's. Mom paid him to take me places when she had to work.

"She is not weird," I said. Even now, I didn't like him criticizing Jane-Marie.

"She was always giggling for no reason," Jason said.

"She was funny," I said. "We told jokes. We laughed a lot."

"Like Matheson and me," Jason said. Chris Matheson was a friend of Jason's. They were always karate-chopping each other. Once they glued their hands together to see what would happen. The nurse in the emergency room had to use nail polish remover to unstick them.

"Is he your best friend?" I asked.

Jason sighed. "Guys don't have best friends."

I knew what he meant. Boys acted like they didn't care who they ate lunch with. They weren't interested in what anybody's favorite food was. They didn't tell each other's secrets.

Actually, I wasn't sure that boys had secrets. But if they did, they didn't blab them around.

We stopped for the light. Jason stuffed his hands

in his pockets. I knew he was trying to think of something to talk about besides his friends.

"So what'd she do, anyway?" he asked. "Kill someone?"

"She told everyone I wanted Katie Kempo to like me," I said.

While I was saying it, I was thinking that when Jane-Marie told my secret, I felt almost as bad as if she had killed someone.

"Aw, man!" Jason looked disgusted. He started walking faster, as if he didn't want to be seen with me. "Girls are so weird!" I heard him say.

"It was a secret!" I said, running to catch up. "One best friend is never supposed to tell another best friend's secret."

Jason just shook his head.

"Don't you have secrets?" I asked.

Jason looked as if he had an itch.

"I guess," he said.

"So what would you do if Chris—if Matheson—told anyone?"

"Why would I go and tell Matheson?" Jason asked. "Then they wouldn't be secrets anymore."

I had never thought about that before.

"I mean," said Jason, "if you don't want anyone to know, don't tell anyone."

But if you didn't tell secrets, I thought, then you never got to know the feeling of someone trusting you most of all.

Suddenly I saw Katie Kempo walking toward us. My heart jumped up into my throat. I had avoided her all day. Now there was no escape.

"Hi, Carolyn," she said. She was smiling. Like she meant it.

"Hi," I said.

"Have you signed up for softball?" she asked.

"Not yet," I said.

"You have to sign up by Friday," Katie said. "Maybe we'll be on the same team."

"Yeah," I said.

Katie Kempo had never said more than one sentence at a time to me in her life. What was this? Was this some kind of joke?

"See you tomorrow," Katie said. She was still smiling. Still like she meant it.

"Wasn't that Kempo?" Jason asked as we turned the corner.

"Mm hm."

"See?" Jason said. "Your problems are solved."

I knew he was trying to be nice. He wanted everything to be OK.

But I was barely listening.

"This proves it," I said. "Katie definitely knows my secret. She wants me to think she likes me, so I'll make an even bigger fool of myself trying to be friends with her."

"You aren't weird," Jason said. "You're nuts."

"Then, when I least expect it, she'll do something horrible," I said. I was starting to panic. "She'll tell everyone she never liked me anyway. She'll tell the whole school," I said, "and we'll have to move."

"Weird *and* nuts," said Jason. He looked fed up. "Maybe nobody cares about your dumb old secret except you. Maybe Kempo just likes you, that's all. Did you ever think of that?" He opened the door to Miss Ludlow's. "Maybe she's even weirder than you are."

I thought about it all through ballet. Was Jason right about Katie? Did she really just like me? What if we got to be friends?

And what if it was all because Jane-Marie told my secret?

4.
Getting the Hang of It

By the next morning, I knew what I had to do.

"You look determined," Mom said, stirring oat-meal.

"I have a plan," I said.

"Oh, brother," Jason said.

"What kind of plan?" Mom asked.

"A dumb girl plan," Jason said. Sam laughed and smashed a piece of banana into his ear.

I didn't care. I was ready.

No matter how nice she was, I wouldn't be nice back.

But it was hard.

"Yecch! Ham again," Katie said, peeking into her sandwich. She looked across at me. "What do you have?"

"Turkey," I said. I tried not to look too friendly.

"Ooh, turkey! Do you want to trade, Carolyn? Please?"

"OK." I liked ham better than turkey anyway.

Katie took a bite of my sandwich. "So what position do you like?"

"What?" I was concentrating so hard on not being nice that I didn't hear her.

"I play shortstop," Katie said.

"Oh," I said. "Right field."

"I have trouble with pop flies," Katie said.

"Fly balls are easy," I said. I hoped I sounded cool. Katie looked away.

I hated hurting someone's feelings. Even someone who was going to laugh at me in front of the whole school. "But I always miss grounders," I said. "I'm terrible at those."

Katie looked relieved. "Maybe we could practice together after school," she said.

"Maybe," I said. I thought a minute. "As long as we don't have to have celery and peanut butter for a snack."

I hoped she wouldn't ask me why.

Katie thought, too. Then she said, "How about carrot muffins and buttermilk?"

We both said "Yecch!" at the same time and laughed. And that was when I knew. I knew that Katie didn't know my secret. Or if she did, she didn't care.

And I knew something else. That someday she would sneak a look at me and say, "How about carrot muffins and buttermilk?" And that we would laugh until our stomachs ached.

That was about a month ago. It's been hard to make myself not wonder about Jane-Marie. I almost called her up to ask if she got the leotards I knew she wanted. Just so I could stop thinking about it.

But I didn't.

Today, I was eating with Eleanor when Jane-Marie and Ruth Houlihan sat down. Ruth is Jane-Marie's new best friend. She always gets picked first for teams. Now Jane-Marie gets picked next.

Jane-Marie took a bite of her tuna sandwich. Jane-Marie hates tuna, I thought. Or used to.

A lot can change in a month.

"How's softball?" she asked.

"Good," I said. "Our pitching stinks, though."

It felt funny to be talking to Jane-Marie as if nothing had happened.

Jane-Marie nodded.

"I hear Katie's a pretty good shortstop," she said.

"Yeah," I said.

"I never meant to tell," Jane-Marie said.

Just like that.

I looked at Eleanor and Ruth. They were watching fifth graders throw food. They weren't paying any attention to us.

"I tried to write you a note," she said. "I wrote it about ten times." She sighed. "It just wouldn't come out right."

I thought of Eleanor trying to figure out subtraction. It's too bad best friends don't have rules to follow, I thought.

Jane-Marie picked up her sandwich. Then she put it down without taking a bite.

"I'm sorry," she said.

"OK," I said.

And for the first time in about a month, it almost was.

Almost.

"You tell me a secret," I said to Jane-Marie.

"What?"

"Tell me a secret," I said. "Something important."

Jane-Marie thought for a while. Then she leaned across the table and whispered, "I guess I was jealous."

"What do you mean?"

"Of you wanting Katie to like you," Jane-Marie said. "I didn't want you to want any other friends. I guess—" She stopped and thought. "I wanted to be the only one."

Finally I said, "You're the only one who calls me CB."

Jane-Marie looked cheered up.

"But I like Katie. You were wrong about her," I said. "And Eleanor." I thought about how to say it. "I don't want to just stop liking them."

"I know," Jane-Marie said.

"I like eating lunch with different people every day," I said. "I like laughing at different people's jokes."

I watched Jane-Marie. She looked disappointed. But she didn't look mad.

The bell rang. Jane-Marie snapped her lunchbox shut.

"Want to walk home with me today, CB?"

"Yeah," I said. "That would be fun."

I'd missed being called CB.

I slurped up the last of my juice and stood up.

"Remember," Jane-Marie whispered. "It was a secret. About my being jealous. You said for it to be a secret. So don't tell anyone."

"I *know*," I said. I am a good secret-keeper. Katie told me she lets her cat sleep in bed with her even though her mother thinks he sleeps outside. She told me not to tell, so I won't, even though I don't think it's a very interesting secret.

"CB?"

"Yeah?"

"If you want to tell me any secrets," Jane-Marie said, "I promise I won't tell." She made an X over her chest with her finger. "I promise, promise, promise."

I believed her.

"Maybe soon," I said.

No matter what Jason says, I miss having a friend I can tell secrets to. I miss trusting someone most of all.

Mom would say, it's complicated. Remembering and laughing and secrets. And she's right. Being a best friend is the most complicated thing I've ever done.

But maybe, with just the right best friends, I will start to get the hang of it.

Gina Willner-Pardo received a bachelor's degree from Bryn Mawr College and a master's degree from the University of California at Berkeley. She has worked as an editor and now writes full time. Her previous books for Clarion are *What I'll Remember When I Am a Grownup*, which *Kirkus Reviews* called "a clear, well-crafted narrative . . . likably authentic," and *Jason and the Losers*. Ms. Willner-Pardo lives in California with her husband and their two children.

Nancy Poydar has degrees in English literature and education from Tufts University. She taught elementary school for twenty years, then took a class in children's book illustration and took a year off to put together a portfolio. "I was hooked months before my first assignment," she says. She is now the highly regarded illustrator of more than a dozen books for children. This is her first for Clarion. Ms. Poydar lives in Wayland, Massachusetts, with her husband.

JEF
WIL

Willner-Pardo, Gina

When Jane-Marie told
my secret

$14.95

DATE			